INSPIRED BY A TRUE STORY

The Old Ways

SUSAN MARGARET CHAPMAN

Illustrated by
JOHN MANTHA

FIFTH
HOUSE

Published in Canada by Fifth House Publishers, 195 Allstate Parkway, Markham, ON, L3R 4T8
www.fitzhenry.ca
Published in the U.S. by Fifth House Publishers, 311 Washington Street, Brighton,
Massachusetts 02135

We acknowledge with thanks the Canada Council for the Arts, and the Ontario Arts Council
for their support of our publishing program. We acknowledge the financial support of the
Government of Canada through the Canada Book Fund (CBF) for our publishing activities.

Library and Archives Canada Cataloguing in Publication
ISBN 978-1-92708-316-1 (bound)
Data available on file

Publisher Cataloging-in-Publication Data (U.S.)
ISBN 978-1-92708-316-1 (bound)
Data available on file

Text and cover design by Kong Njo
Cover illustration courtesy of John Mantha

Printed and bound in Canada by Friesens Corporation

FOR KEN

With thanks to Ataguttaluk Elementary School,
Igloolik, Nunavut

Simon jumped off his skis and ran into the house. His fingers were numb, and the warmth of the stove felt good. His grandma smiled. "Good day at school?"

Simon nodded. "I got to use the computer today, Ananaksaq."

Ananaksaq shook her head. "Computers," she said, as she poured him some hot, milky tea.

"What's for dinner?"
Simon had hoped for pizza,
or macaroni and cheese, but
he could already smell caribou
stew. His grandma sipped her
tea while Simon told her all
about his day. "We saw a movie
this morning. It was great!"

"What was it about?"

"A magic fish . . . that grants a
fisherman some wishes."

That reminded Simon's
grandma of an old story about
Sedna, the goddess of the sea,
and she started to tell it.

Simon jumped up impatiently.
"Sorry, but my show is on,
Ananaksaq." He hurried to
turn on the TV.

After his show Ananaksaq said, "Homework time." Simon opened his backpack and started his math.

Before long, Simon's grandpa stomped through the doorway, shaking off the snow. "Would you like me to show you how to build an igloo today?" he asked. "The snow is perfect."

Simon sighed. *Ataatga and the old ways again.*

"No thanks, Ataatga," said Simon. "I was just going to play my video game."

His grandpa looked disappointed. "Video games," he said. "Well, maybe another time." Then he brightened. "Tomorrow we are going

to Aunt Mary and Uncle John's in Igloolik for Aunt Mary's birthday dinner. It's just a short snowmobile ride."

Simon grinned. Aunt Mary's big family was fun. They always danced and sang and played games.

In the morning Simon watched his grandpa getting ready. Ataatga attached a sled to the snowmobile and loaded some big leather bags onto it. Simon heard the clanking of tools and knives from inside one of the bags. Then his grandpa added a large gas tank and a container of oil. Ananaksaq got the warm caribou parkas and put them on the sled. Finally, she brought out a box of food to take to Aunt Mary's.

Ataatga piled some snowshoes on top, covered everything with caribou skins, and tied it all down.

"Why do we need all this, Ataatga?" Simon asked. "You said it won't take us very long to get there."

"You never know," said his grandpa. "We have to be prepared for anything."

Silly, thought Simon. *Ataatga is still stuck in the old ways. Well, not me.* Simon began dreaming of the new video game he wanted for his birthday.

Everything was ready, and they set off. It was cold and blowing a
bit. Snow swirled in a little round pattern in front of them. Suddenly
Ataatga stopped the snowmobile. "Open water," he muttered. "We'll
have to take the long trail." He veered off in another direction.

They drove in silence for an hour, when there was a loud bang. The snowmobile stopped. Ataatga jumped off and tinkered with the motor. Nothing. There were two frown lines between his eyes. The snow was blowing harder. Simon couldn't even see the tracks of the snowmobile now.

"We're in for it," said Ataatga. He wrapped Ananaksaq and Simon in the caribou skins from the sled. Then he opened a bag and took out his snow knife. He cut snow blocks and placed them in a circle. He placed a second layer on top, a little bit smaller. Slowly the walls went up and curved over Ataatga's head. He left a smoke hole at the top.

Ataatga asked Simon to stuff snow all around the blocks to make sure no cold air could get in. He told Simon to leave one bottom block so that it could be used for a door. They all crawled inside. Ataatga brought in a seal oil lamp and lit it. Simon was surprised at how much heat it gave off. Soon the igloo felt warm and comfortable.

"I'm hungry," whispered Simon. His grandma brought the box of food from outside and made some bannock. She cooked it over the flame, and handed it to Simon. Then she melted some snow for tea. Simon settled down in the caribou skins. There was nothing to do. *I wish there was a TV*, he thought.

Ananaksaq started to tell a story. It was all about a woman who adopted a polar bear as her son. This time Simon listened. He could see the story in his head. Ataatga was listening too. And so, tired and warm, Simon dozed off. He dreamed of polar bears flying through the sky.

Simon woke up a short time later to the sound of low voices.

"It's still too risky to go for help, and I don't want to leave you both alone," Ataaga told Ananaksaq. "We'll wait till the storm stops."

Simon's stomach skittered. *How will we ever get home?* he wondered.

Ananaksaq told another story. This one was funny – about why the raven is black and the loon is speckled. Simon laughed and felt better. Ananaksaq heated up the caribou stew she had brought. Simon dipped his bannock into the gravy and wolfed every bit of it down. It tasted better than ever before. Finally, he slept, wrapped in dreams and caribou skins.

In the morning, they crawled out of the tunnel. The storm had stopped. The snowmobile was covered in snow. Ataatga tried to start it. Nothing. "Uncle John will find us soon," he said. "We'll just wait."

So they waited all day, but no one came. Ataatga kept going outside to check the skyline. Night fell, and they finished off the rest of the stew.

Simon's grandparents looked worried. There was no more food. But they were warm. And Ananaksaq had more stories. And another day was coming.

The next morning, Ataatga went outside and gazed at the empty horizon again. "They must be looking on the other trails," he said. He got out his compass. "It's about twenty kilometres to Igloolik. I'll start walking. There are lots of inuksuit on this trail to show me the way."

Simon was afraid. He felt safe when his grandpa was there.

"You'll be fine," said Ataatga. "You are warm and dry. I'll be back soon with help. Be brave for your grandma."

Ataatga strapped on his snowshoes and crunched away, into the flat horizon.

Simon and his grandma went back inside the igloo. Ananaksaq told many tales that morning. They helped him to forget how hungry he was. He heard about the crow who brought light to the North. Simon was lost in a world of magic and history. And the hours went by. And his stomach growled.

Ananaksaq looked tired, and she was running out of stories. So Simon told her the story of the magic fish from the movie at school. He tried to make it really interesting the way she did. He changed his voice and waved his arms. Ananaksaq smiled and gave him a hug. "You are a great storyteller," she told him.

The sun was sliding lower in the sky when they heard a shout. They scrambled out of the igloo. Two snowmobiles hummed toward them, with Ataatga on one and Uncle John on the other.

Quickly they packed everything onto the sled and attached it to one snowmobile. They hooked up the broken snowmobile to the other, and set off, with Simon sitting behind his grandpa and Ananaksaq behind Uncle John.

When they arrived at Aunt Mary's, everyone was there to greet them. As his grandpa lifted him off the snowmobile, Simon said, "Ataatga, I think I would like to learn more about the old ways. Tomorrow will you show me again how to build an igloo?"

Simon's grandpa smiled a very big smile. "You bet I will!" he said.